ARIKI
and the
ISLAND OF WONDERS

**WALKER
BOOKS**

First published 2019 by Walker Books Ltd
87 Vauxhall Walk, London SE11 5HJ

2 4 6 8 10 9 7 5 3 1

Text © 2019 Nicola Davies
Illustrations © 2019 Nicola Kinnear

The right of Nicola Davies and Nicola Kinnear to be identified as
author and illustrator respectively of this work has been asserted by them
in accordance with the Copyright, Designs and Patents Act 1988

This book has been typeset in Veronan

Printed and bound in Great Britain
by CPI Group (UK) Ltd, Croydon CR0 4YY

British Library Cataloguing in Publication Data:
a catalogue record for this book is available from the British Library

ISBN 978-1-4063-6980-9

www.walker.co.uk

For Poppy Bradbury – officially Ariki's biggest fan
Nicola Davies

For my Grandad, Robert
Nicola Kinnear

We are used to thinking of the sea as something that you get to when the land runs out. But just suppose you lived the other way round, in a place where sea stretched from one horizon to the other and land was very hard to find…

This is not an imaginary place. If you look at a map of the world you can find it, that big expanse of ocean we call the Pacific. A whole world of water dotted with the smallest scraps of land.

Long ago, a girl lived there, on a tiny island shaped like a sea turtle. She rode on the tails of sharks; she used the stars as stepping stones; she sang songs to the storm. But most of all, she knew what it meant to live in the true colour of our planet – which is not green, but blue.

Her name was Ariki and this is one of her adventures.

CHAPTER 1

It was a beautiful day on Turtle Island. The late afternoon sun slanted golden through the treetops, and the breeze made the palm leaves shimmer and dance. There was no sign of the big storms that sometimes came at this season, just a few, well-behaved little clouds dawdling along the horizon, promising a nice cooling shower before morning. The sea glowed the perfect shade of deep turquoise – Ariki's favourite colour. How she longed to be out on that delicious blueness! She would paddle her canoe from the little cove called the Turtle's Neck;

she could almost hear the soft slapping sound of the waves against its wooden side...

"Are you paying attention?" the stern voice of her guardian Arohaka brought her back to reality. "Paying attention is the first and most important skill of the Star Walker. You will never learn to be a Master Navigator without it."

Ariki sighed. She wanted to learn, she really did – she'd even cut off her long hair so it wouldn't get in the way. But being an apprentice Star Walker was not quite what she had expected it to be. She had imagined going on long sea voyages and steering a course by new stars, visiting islands that spouted fire and finding the place, far, far away, from where she had come ... not sitting in the gloom of the Gathering Hut, staring at stones.

"We have covered three new constellations today," said Arohaka, pointing to the pebbles on the sandy floor that represented the patterns of stars in

the sky. "I expect you to know those by tomorrow. Now we will move on to wave patterns."

The old man knelt beside a large bowl of water on the ground, and began to poke its surface with a twig. "Observe the ripples," he said. "This is how you will learn about the behaviour of waves."

Ariki knelt beside him, staring in disbelief at the bowl. Was he, Master Navigator and famous Star Walker, suggesting she learned about the ocean from a *dish*, when the real ocean was right there, peeping at her between the coconut palms? She gazed out at it; she could almost feel it calling to her.

Arohaka snapped his long fingers in front of her nose. "Stop daydreaming, Ariki."

She knew she must try harder. She had swum with a giant shark to prove herself worthy to be Arohaka's apprentice and she wanted him to believe in her. But this was so hard.

"I just want to be on the ocean," she said.

The old man sighed, and laid a hand lightly on her head. "I know, I know. But this knowledge might save your life one day. So *concentrate!*"

Arohaka placed a round pebble at one end of the shallow, water-filled bowl, then jiggled the twig at the other end to make a series of little waves that bounced back and bent round the pebble.

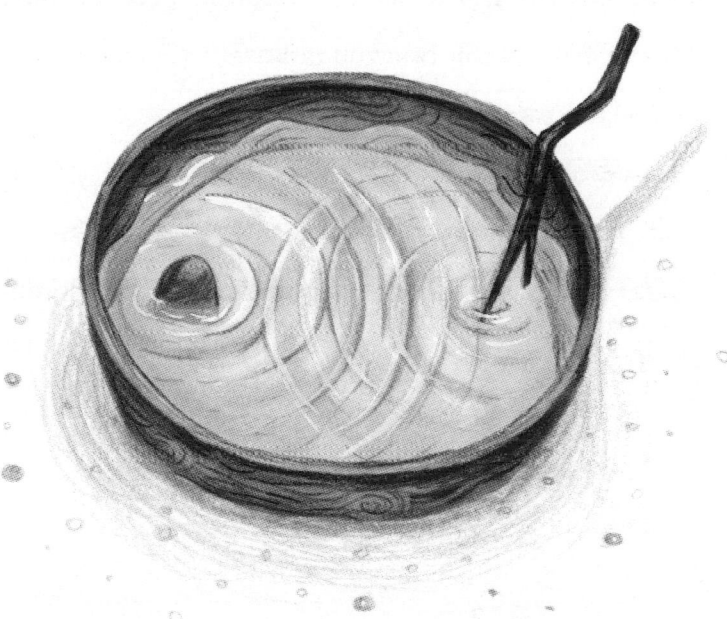

"This is how waves reflect from an island and flow around it," he said. "You can find an island from waves like this, even when it is out of sight over the horizon."

He put another pebble in the pool, then handed her the twig and a bunch of dried grass straws.

"I have business to attend to. When I get back, I want to see a precise model of the ripple patterns around these pebbles made with the straws. No running off today," he warned sternly. "You will be a Master Navigator, but you must study."

Ariki watched the tall, straight figure of the old Star Walker disappear between the tree trunks. Her pet pig Bad Boy, seeming to sense that the day might finally get a little more interesting, suddenly woke up.

"Snrt?" he said hopefully.

Ariki shook her head. "No time to play yet," she told him. "Go back to sleep."

But Bad Boy was ready for a game. He trotted over from the patch of sunlight where he had been snoozing and looked up at Ariki with his most mischievous expression: eyes twinkling, ears wiggling. It was irresistible.

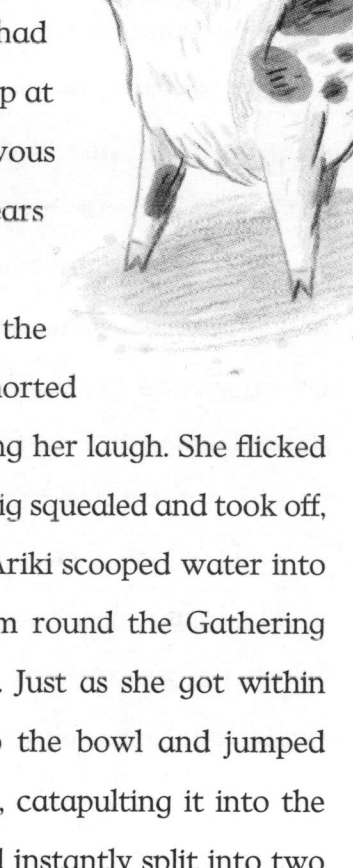

Ariki flicked water from the bowl onto his nose. He snorted and stamped his feet, making her laugh. She flicked some more water, and the pig squealed and took off, his tail twirling in delight. Ariki scooped water into both hands and chased him round the Gathering Hut, trying to shower him. Just as she got within range, he doubled back to the bowl and jumped on the edge with both feet, catapulting it into the air. It landed on its side and instantly split into two neat halves, which came to rest on either side of the soggy, and now useless, straws.

Ariki and Bad Boy stared at the muddy mess they had created. Arohaka wouldn't be gone long, and when he came back he would be very cross.

Ariki shoved the remains of the bowl and the soggy straws into a dark corner. Maybe if she speared a fish for her guardian's dinner then he wouldn't be quite so angry about the broken bowl and her neglect of her studies. She grabbed her new fishing spear – the one studded with a row of small, sharp shark teeth – and ran out into the sunshine with Bad Boy at her heels.

It was so good to be outside! Ariki was about to jump into her canoe when she thought of her best friend, Ipo. Ipo was a young artist whose beautiful designs were in great demand. For the last few weeks he'd been too busy to come fishing and Ariki couldn't help feeling that it was partly her fault.

She had solved the mystery of the giant shark that was terrifying the Islanders, by working out that all it wanted was a safe place to have its pups. Then, when the pups were born, an amazing thing happened. It turned out their skins had the same black and white pattern as her own tattoos. Those patterns had always marked Ariki as different – she was the strange girl who had washed ashore as a toddler, from who knew where. Now, the tattoos were part of a story everyone wanted to hear – and to record by painting some scene from the story on the bark cloth of their best clothes. Poor Ipo was working *all* the time.

He definitely deserved a break, and Ariki was going to make him take one. She turned from the beach and slipped back through the trees.

"Stay close!" she told Bad Boy. "We don't want Arohaka to spot us."

Ipo worked under the big thatched awning that his granny had built next to their house. During the day, he had to keep out of the bright sun because he had been born as white as a shell, and his skin burned in bright light. But everyone enjoyed a bit of shade, so he was rarely short of company as he worked. People stood around, chatting and watching all that was going on along Turtle Back beach: net-mending, fish trap-making, boat-building, baby cuddling, paddling, swimming, plus all the comings and goings of boats heading up or down the Nose – the narrow channel in the reef that linked the lagoon with the open sea.

This afternoon, to Ariki's delight, Ipo was alone.

"*Pssst*," she hissed from behind a tree.

Ipo looked up, pushing a cloud of snowy white hair out of his eyes.

"Hiding from Arohaka again?" He grinned. "Come and sit. Everyone's at the Queen's house talking about the wedding." Ipo rolled his eyes.

The Queen of Turtle Island, Manatui, was getting married to the eldest son of the Queen of Big Toe, an island three days' journey away across the sea

– their closest neighbour. Turtle Island grown-ups had talked about nothing but the wedding feast for weeks. It was *very* dull.

Ariki plopped down on the sand beside her friend, while Bad Boy snuffled around on the floor for bits of dried fish or coconut.

"We did looking at pebbles *again* today," she grumbled, "and then looking at ripples in a bowl. If I don't get on the ocean soon I'm going to go mad. Come fishing with me!"

"I can't," Ipo groaned. "The daughters of the Queen of Big Toe are visiting and I have to get their outfits done by morning."

Ariki glanced down at the huge area of cloth. "These are *skirts*?"

Ipo nodded.

"Wow, I thought they were tents."

"They wanted them extra swirly, to make room for designs." Ipo sighed. "It's a lot of work."

As if hearing themselves mentioned, three young women with very elaborate hairdos emerged from the house of Queen Manatui and came rushing along the beach towards them, their shell necklaces jangling.

"Oh! Oh, it's *her*," the one on the left exclaimed.

"It is!" cried the one on the right. "The *real* Ariki."

They squealed like piglets.

"Amazing," said the one in the middle.

"I'm sorry," Ipo whispered. "I should have warned you..."

Before Ariki could escape, the three sisters had her surrounded and were looking at her as if she were some kind of special ingredient in their favourite meal.

"Just look at those weird tattoos," the first one said, poking Ariki in the arm.

"And on the *boys'* side. How strange," said the second, stretching out her arm to show off her "normal" tattoos – swirls and curves painted on her right arm, the "girls' side".

"Amazing," commented the third, again.

Ariki glanced between the girls to see if she could make a run for it and instead spotted a beautiful boat, with a smooth hull and graceful outrigger, a deck with a cabin and a bright new sail. It was, she guessed, the boat the three young women had arrived in. It gave her an idea.

"Would you like to hear about my meeting with the Giant Shark," she said, "at the place where it actually happened?"

"Oh," said the first one.

"Yes!" said the second.

The third struggled to answer. "That would be ...

be…" she stuttered.

"Amazing?" Ariki suggested and they all nodded.
"Good." She beamed. "Can we go in your boat?"

The girls looked at one another rather uncertainly,
then nodded all together.

"It's new," the first girl said proudly. "Our mother
had it built."

"She named it *Sea Beauty*," said the second,
patting her hair, "after us!"

"Oh," said Ariki. "That's nice."

Ipo looked at Ariki with a "What are you up
to?" expression on his face, but Ariki just smiled
innocently.

"Come on, Ipo," she said. "You can take a little
break, can't you, now the sun is going down?"

Ipo hesitated, but only for a moment. He grabbed
his sunhat, with its extra-wide brim, and followed
his friend down the beach.

It was obvious that, as the girls were older and

stronger, they should be the ones to push *Sea Beauty* out into the waves, while Ipo, Ariki and Bad Boy sat on board, and paddled to get it moving.

The moment the boat floated free of the sand, Ariki felt it come to life under her feet – like a fish suddenly released from a net. It was thrilling! The breeze that earlier had been ruffling the palms had picked up, so when Ariki released the sail, perhaps just a little too early, *Sea Beauty* leaped away before the Queen's daughters could climb aboard. The boat raced from the shore as if it longed for freedom as much as Ariki did.

"I'm so sorry," Ariki called over her shoulder to the girls now standing chest-deep in water. "We'll take her out a bit and turn her round."

"Ariki," said Ipo, "you planned that."

"No I didn't! The wind was stronger than I expected. But now we've got her, let's just take her for a little spin?"

"We'll be in trouble..." Ipo said.

"We will," Ariki agreed.

And then they smiled at each other and shot
out through the Nose into the ocean.

CHAPTER 2

Like most Turtle Island children, Ariki had swum, paddled canoes and sailed before she could walk. Ipo's need to keep out of strong sunlight had given him a late start on the sea, so he was a little less skilled and a lot more cautious.

But today the two friends were too excited to be cautious. They had never sailed a boat like this before. Usually children got the old or broken crafts, those discarded as too slow or unreliable on long voyages. *Sea Beauty* was very different. Her crisp white sail was shaped like a crab's claw, and edged with painted patterns: magic charms to keep her safe at sea. Her hull and outrigger were as smooth and sleek as barracuda. They were joined by a deck with a small cabin on top, made of woven palm. All her ropes were new and neat, with not a single fray.

Ipo steered, leaning into the long paddle that acted as a rudder to keep *Sea Beauty* slicing through the choppy water. Ariki handled the sail, hauling the ropes to change its angle and get the most out of the wind.

"It's like sailing a dolphin!" Ipo cried.

"Or being one," said Ariki.

The dolphins seemed to agree, because for a few minutes a little pod joined them, riding their bow wave. Bad Boy was fascinated and stared down at them through the water.

"Maybe he thinks they're underwater pigs." Ipo laughed.

Bad Boy grunted loudly as the dolphins shot away and disappeared into the blue.

It felt wonderful to be zipping along in such a perfect boat. They were so caught up in making *Sea Beauty* go as fast as possible that they didn't notice the sea becoming darker; they didn't look behind them, to where the sky had changed colour – as if a huge fist had punched the heavens and left a bruise.

But pigs are good at smelling bad weather. Bad Boy was the first to sense the danger; he snorted and stamped in alarm. Ipo turned to look behind them and gasped as the wind gusted and tore off his special sunhat, sending it flying over the sea.

"Look, Ariki. Look!" he cried.

Ariki heard the fear in her friend's voice and glanced round. In a short time they had travelled a long way: Turtle Island was just a green smudge on the horizon, which Ariki could cover with her thumb. Behind it was the biggest, most evil-looking storm cloud she had ever seen, deep grey and purple, shot through with sparks of lightning. Already the sea was marked with white-topped waves and sheets of rain were drawing grey curtains between them and the shore.

"Turn around!" Ariki cried. "We'll have to try to get home before the wind is too strong."

But even as she said it, Ariki knew it was already too late. The sea that had been a friendly blue such a short time ago had turned dark and grown teeth. They fought against the wind and the waves that grew stronger every moment – and got nowhere. There was only one thing to do: run before the storm and let it blow them where it wanted.

"I'm taking her round," Ipo shouted over the roar of the wind.

"Ready," Ariki called.

Ipo pushed the rudder and the lovely boat turned gratefully away from her head-on battle. But at that moment, all the charms painted on her sail failed her; the wind punched harder than before, the waves

struck like hammer blows and suddenly Ariki and Ipo found themselves underwater – the beautiful boat had been tipped upside down.

For a moment, Ariki struggled to understand what had happened. Bad Boy floated past her, his little feet a blur of paddling as he struggled for air: she pulled him under her arm and, clutching a trailing rope in her other hand, kicked for the surface. She couldn't see Ipo anywhere, just a mass of foam and green waves swirling round the upturned boat. If he had been washed away from *Sea Beauty* she would never find him. But without a boat, neither of them would have a chance of survival – so her first task must be righting *Sea Beauty*.

She part swam, part clambered, until she was under the smaller, outrigger hull. If she could push it up then climb on, her weight should be enough to lever the main hull and the sail out of the water. She slipped the loop of rope round Bad Boy's middle and hoped he could stay afloat for long enough … then she pushed with all her might!

The timbers and ropes groaned and grumbled, but the outrigger popped up. That was the easy part. Ariki climbed onto it and hung from its outer edge, swinging her whole weight to try and lever the main hull upright. She felt that her arms would break; her fingers began to lose their grip. Another few minutes and the wind and waves would start to pull *Sea Beauty* apart. Then, above her, she heard a snort – somehow Bad Boy had managed to climb aboard. He stood on the outrigger and looked down at her as she dangled, as if he knew his extra weight was just enough to make the difference. With a final judder, *Sea Beauty* plopped upright and Ariki scrambled onto the deck.

And there was Ipo. Clinging on, wedged beside the rudder, coughing and spluttering but clearly very much alive. Ariki felt a hot pulse of relief pass through her body as she helped him up onto the deck. He had a big gash on his forehead, but there was no time to worry about that now.

"I'll lash the rudder so it'll hold," Ipo shouted above the noise of the storm.

"Good plan," Ariki yelled back: tied tightly in one position, it might stop them from capsizing again.

She went back to the prow to secure the sail. Half of the fabric of the beautiful crab's claw sail had been ripped away, but its stiff frame was still intact. Ariki struggled with the tangled ropes, but managed to rig what remained of the sail so it would offer the storm wind the smallest area; just enough to keep them moving but not enough for the wind to tear to bits. With the broken sail set and the rudder lashed, there was nothing more they could do but huddle in the little cabin with the shuddering Bad Boy between them, and hope that the ocean would spare their lives.

Rain whipped down; wind beat the sea into lines of flying foam; waves grew until *Sea Beauty* was sliding up and down the sides of moving mountains of water. Down in the troughs they had a few moments of peace, with just a little shelter, but up on the wave peaks they were battered by the full force of the storm. In the eerie twilight, under the swirling clouds, it was hard to tell what was sea and what was sky.

Night came, a dark so deep they were unable even to see each other's frightened faces. Only the pulse in her wrist told Ariki that time had not frozen. At last there was a pale grey glimmer of dawn, but the storm still raged. Sometime, Ariki couldn't remember when, she struggled on deck to collect rainwater trickling down the sail; a little salty but fresh enough to keep them alive.

Dark returned. They told stories for comfort, speaking right into each other's ears to be heard above the waves and wind,

"Maybe Paikea the Whale Queen will come and save us," Ipo said.

"Like in the song?"

"Yes. The one where she tows the canoe of Princess Hamui back to her home island."

Ariki squeezed his hand. "Maybe," she said. "Maybe."

The boat was driven over the mountains and valleys of the ocean much faster than they could ever have sailed. How far would it take them? Would they ever make it back?

CHAPTER 3

The light was blinding, hot and white, burning through Ariki's eyelids. Something was trying to eat her hair, so she peeped between her fingers at two beady eyes and a flat, round nose.

"*Snff,*" said Bad Boy. "*Snnnnffff!*"

"Hello," said Ariki. "Well, nice to see you too." She scratched the piglet behind the ears and his tail twirled a little, but he didn't get up. On the other side of her, Ipo was still asleep. The cut on his head had stopped bleeding but a big purple bruise had formed around it and his lips looked dry and cracked.

He needed water. They all needed water. Ariki was so thirsty her mouth burned.

She got to her feet and wobbled out on deck. No wind. No rain. No clouds or lightning. Nothing but blue sky and blue sea. Nothing at all.

The storm had blown for days and taken them a great distance to the west, at such speed that their return journey would take far longer. But now Ariki saw that their rudder was broken, their extra paddles gone and all that was left of the sail was a long, limp ribbon of cloth. They were drifting on empty ocean, with no way to move in any direction. To have a chance of getting home, or even surviving the next few days, they had to find an island. But Ariki had never heard of any islands in this part of the ocean.

She searched the boat for anything that might help them. Wedged into the prow of the outrigger she found a gourd, half full of rainwater, and an oiled leather bag with some dried breadfruit inside. Perhaps their luck had not altogether run out. She took them back to the cabin and shared the food and water with Ipo and Bad Boy, who were just waking up and blinking in the light.

"Well, apprentice Star Walker," said Ipo, "where d'you think we are?"

"About five days west of Turtle," Ariki said, trying to sound more certain than she was. "I'll know more tonight, when I can see the stars."

"Why wasn't it a westerly storm?" Ipo sighed. "It

would have blown us all the way to my great-uncle's island."

It was true: a storm from any other direction would have blown them close to a dozen different island clusters they often visited for fishing, trade or to see relatives. But no one ever came to this bit of ocean.

"How much water is there?" Ipo asked. Ariki shook the gourd in answer. "A mouthful for five days' journey? We'd better hope it rains." Ipo sank back onto the floor of the hut and closed his eyes.

Ariki left Ipo and Bad Boy resting and sat with her feet dangling over the side of the boat. Had they simply exchanged a quick death by drowning for a slow one from thirst and hunger? Their only hope was that there might be an island to the west, hiding just over the horizon – close enough to save them. She scanned the sea and the sky for clues: birds flying out from their nests on some tiny, forgotten scrap of land; leaves or twigs blown from nearby trees; a tell-tale cloud sitting high over an island.

There was nothing at all, except the last remnant of the storm, a steady line of waves pacing over the ocean from east to west, bobbing *Sea Beauty* gently up and down, up and down.

Then Ariki noticed that there was another rhythm in the waves. She stared at the water, but she couldn't quite make it out. Perhaps if she was *in* the water, it would be clearer. Holding on to the outrigger with one hand, she dropped over the side.

Immediately, she felt better and more hopeful. She closed her eyes and tuned her senses to the feel of the water on her skin.

There was the pattern of the storm swell, hitting one side of her body like a slow drum beat.

And *there* was the other beat, just a little faster, much weaker, but coming from the other side;

tiny waves travelling in the opposite direction. She could feel them flowing past her body and when she opened her eyes, right at the surface, she could see them. A faint train of tiny waves criss-crossing the storm swell. Just like the ripples bouncing off the pebble in Arohaka's dish! Somewhere to the west, out of sight but not so very far off, there was an island – perhaps close enough to get to with a single makeshift paddle.

She pulled herself out of the water and rushed to the cabin where Ipo was hiding from the sun.

"Ipo!" she called out excitedly. "Ripples!"

Ipo sat up. "I thought you said ripples were boring and a waste of time," he said grumpily.

"I was wrong. *These* ripples are showing there's an island – that way."

"That's the opposite way from home, Ariki. Supposing we go that way and there isn't an island?"

"But there *is*."

Ipo shook his head and looked very cross. "What if you're wrong?" he said. "We're in enough trouble already, without going further and further in the wrong direction."

"I'm *not* wrong."

Pwfffffffff! A cloud of vapour exploded into the sunshine right beside the boat and interrupted their disagreement. *Sea Beauty* rocked and sent Ariki sprawling. Bad Boy opened his eyes and oinked faintly in fear.

"It's a whale!" Ariki shouted.

"I can see that," Ipo snapped, "but what's it doing so close to our boat?"

The whale was rubbing the underside of the hull, making *Sea Beauty* shiver and shake. Ariki got down on the outrigger and leaned close to the water to take a look.

"It's a Big-Wing," she called out. "I can see its long flippers."

She peered into the water. There was the
creature's blowhole, just below the surface, and the
two long white flippers like skinny wings, which
gave these whales their name. Its body was as long
as the canoe, but that was small for a Big-Wing.
They sometimes came close to Turtle Island – but
neither she nor Ipo had ever seen one *this* close.

"I think it's a baby," she told Ipo.

"Just let me make a sunshade," Ipo called from the cabin, "and I'll be there!" The whale had obviously made him forget about being cross.

A moment later he was beside her with a large square of palm-matting tied onto his head.

"Nice!" said Ariki.

"It's the best I could do."

Together, the children leaned over the side.

Pwwfff, the whale breathed again. *Pwwff!*

It was dangling in the water, its tail and flippers moving just enough to keep it in one place.

"It's Paikea the Whale Queen, come to save us," Ipo breathed.

He began to sing softly:

"Paikea the Whale Queen
swam to the rescue, and said,
'Princess Hamui, I will tow your canoe
and carry you safe to land once more.'"

Ariki shook her head. "I don't think so." She grinned. "It's too small to be a Whale Queen and I haven't got four arms like Princess Hamui. I think it's hurt, and needs our help."

"Well," said Ipo, "if we help it, then it might help *us*."

"Good idea," Ariki replied. "I'll take a look."

She slid into the water beside the whale very gently, so as not to frighten it. She could see in its eye that it was afraid, but it didn't try to move away. She knew she had to be sensible, but Ipo was right – this *was* like the song!

Ariki spoke to the whale in her head. This was the way she had managed to communicate with the Giant Shark, speaking in her thoughts and then listening for its thoughts to land in her mind. But there was no way of knowing if it would work with a whale.

I know how you feel, she said. *I was lost too, when I was little. I wonder if you're hurt?*

The whale didn't seem to respond, but she swam closer anyway; yes it *was* hurt! She took another breath then dived again for a closer look. Somehow the baby had stabbed itself on a spike of coral: a piece half the length of Ariki's forearm was sticking out of the underside of its tail. Wisps of blood were blossoming around it. Gently, Ariki touched the coral spike.

All right, Baby Paikea, Ariki told the whale in her head, *I'm going to pull that out of you.*

The little whale grew very, very still, as if it understood that Ariki was trying to help.

She grasped the spike. It was sharp and would cut

her hand, but there was no help for that. She pulled hard, harder, and the spike popped out, leaving a jagged flap of skin and quite a bit of bleeding. It was only a matter of time before the blood would attract some nasty attention from sharks, no matter where they were in the ocean.

Ariki popped up to the surface. "It's wounded," she told Ipo. "I can use a bit of my tunic to plug the cut, but it needs something to hold it in place."

"What about that last bit of sail?" Ipo suggested. "It's of no use to us, anyway."

He retrieved the sail and passed it down. Ariki tore a strip from her tunic, and dived again.

She wound the sail around the tunic dressing, hoping that the magic charms on it would help the whale to heal.

As she hauled herself out of the water, the little whale began to swim away.

"Oh no!" Ariki cried; she'd been so certain it was going to help them in return.

"Perhaps in the songs of Paikea, we rescue whales – not the other way round," Ipo said calmly.

But the baby didn't go far. It turned and came back underneath the boat. This time it bumped the bottom gently, then stayed still, resting beside them. Ariki and Ipo smiled at each other.

"Looks like it really is here to help us," said Ipo, "though it's a shame you haven't got four arms like Princess Hamui in the story. They'd be pretty useful…"

They decided to try to get the little whale to tow them, just like Paikea in the song. But first, they needed to get the boat ready. Hope gave them new energy, in spite of the lack of food, water and rest. They saved the broken rudder to use as a makeshift paddle and stowed the water gourd where it could be filled up quickly if there was rain. Bad Boy was suffering badly from the lack of water, and they did all they could to make him safe and comfortable. Last of all they took the best remaining ropes and tied them together to make a long tow line, with a big loop on one end.

All the while, the whale stayed close.

"Now we're ready. But I need to ask its permission first," Ariki said.

"If you can talk to giant sharks," Ipo teased, "I suppose talking to whales is easy!"

Ariki dropped into the water beside the whale with the looped end of the tow rope.

"Baby Paikea," she said out loud in her most respectful voice, "will you tow us to land, where we can find water and food?"

She waited for an answer, but the whale just held still in the water.

"It didn't swim away," Ipo said, "so I think that must mean 'yes'."

Ariki dived and swam along the whale's side. She stroked its jaw and the folded corner of its mouth. Then she put her hand next to one of its eyes and showed it the loop of rope.

I need to put this round one of your flippers, she told it in her head. *I'll take it off if you don't like it, I promise.*

Very gently, she slid the loop over its left flipper – but the whale flinched and threw it off. It swam away a little distance, but turned and came back, and offered its flipper. Ariki slipped on the loop and she floated next to the baby's eye again. They looked at each other for a long time.

Thank you, she told it. *I hope we find your mother too.*

The whale blinked and began beating its tail up and down. It seemed to know at once where it was going and it swam strongly, keeping close to the surface so as not to drag *Sea Beauty* down. The ropes went taut and the boat began to move. Ariki scrambled aboard.

"It isn't taking us home," said Ipo.

He was right: the whale was heading west, not east.

"This is the way the ripples said there was an island," Ariki said.

"Well, I hope you and Paikea are right." Ipo smiled. "It'll make a great new song if you are!"

CHAPTER 4

All afternoon, their whale rescuer swam on. Ariki wondered if, without its mother's milk to nourish it, the baby was as thirsty and hungry as she and Ipo and Bad Boy were. There was just the tiniest bit of water left in the gourd, only enough for them to wet their lips a little every few hours.

Bad Boy was still in the cabin. All he seemed to want to do was sleep, and his breathing was very shallow. Ariki scratched his nose and told him to hang on.

The regular *pwwfff* of the whale's breathing

marked out the time – and, at last, the sun set. Still the little whale swam on, as the stars rose out of the dark horizon.

Now Ariki could see the constellations. Although she was only an apprentice Star Walker, she had already learned how to use stars as they rose and set, one after another, to steer a straight course over the ocean. Every destination had a list of stars to get you there: a Star Path. All the Star Paths that Ariki had learned rose up in her mind as she gazed up into the sky, wondering if, so far from Turtle Island, it would contain constellations she had never seen. But one by one, familiar shapes appeared above her, winking in the darkness like old friends.

Ariki said their names quietly to herself: "Little Orphan, Crab's Claw, Chief's Baler..." There they

all were, just like always. And behind her, already setting in the west, was the little yellow star called Sea Urchin. It was the one that would help to steer them home when the time came.

Right now it would be shining over her guardian's house on Turtle Island. How angry Arohaka would be with her... And he was right. She had behaved foolishly, recklessly, stealing *Sea Beauty*; she had not *paid attention*, she had let the storm catch them unawares. She knew she had done wrong, but it was all because the sea called to her in a way that Arohaka didn't understand. It told her that her real home was somewhere out here – hidden in the unknown wildness of the ocean.

"Stop stargazing," Ipo said suddenly. "We're not moving!"

He was right. The tow rope was slack, but when they pulled it, it was clear that the whale was still attached, although it had stopped swimming. Ariki slipped over the side and followed the rope to where the whale hung in the water. She could just make out its dark outline and the pale wings of its flippers wafting up and down in the swell.

Are you tired? she asked it in her head.

It held out the flipper to which the rope was attached and gave it a slow shake. It was asking for the rope to be removed.

All right, Baby Paikea, she told it in thought, *I'll keep my promise.*

As Ariki slipped the rope off its flipper, a huge whale rose beside the calf, pushing her to one side. Ariki popped up to the surface, and there, in the moonlight, were two whale backs and fins – one large, one small. Their baby had found its mother! Ariki peeped below the surface to catch a glimpse

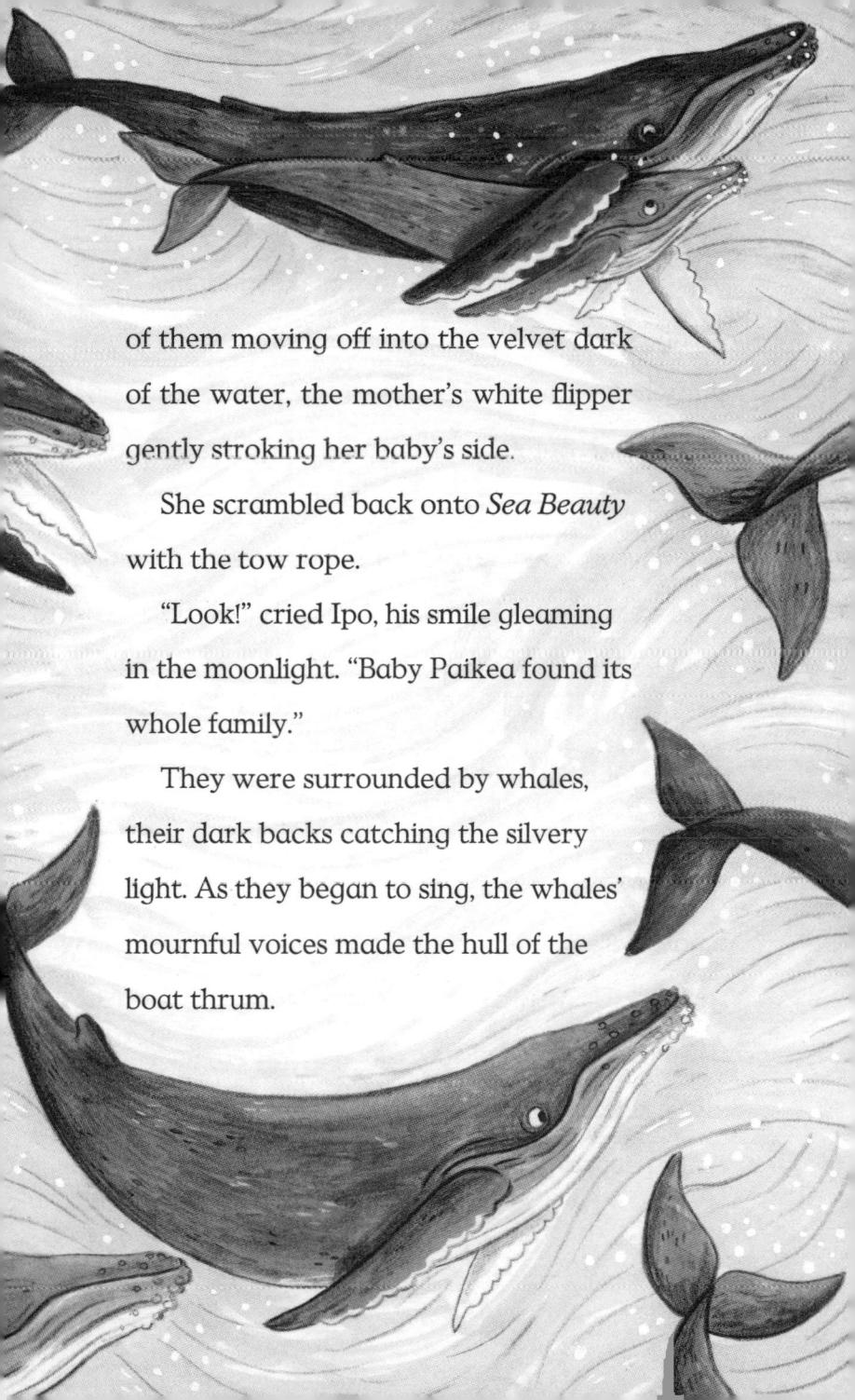

of them moving off into the velvet dark
of the water, the mother's white flipper
gently stroking her baby's side.

She scrambled back onto *Sea Beauty*
with the tow rope.

"Look!" cried Ipo, his smile gleaming
in the moonlight. "Baby Paikea found its
whole family."

They were surrounded by whales,
their dark backs catching the silvery
light. As they began to sing, the whales'
mournful voices made the hull of the
boat thrum.

"*Paikea swam away through the world, singing*,'" said Ipo softly, repeating the final line of the song of Princess Hamui and the Queen of the Whales.

But there was another sound, too: the crash of waves breaking on a reef, far too close for comfort.

"Baby Paikea did bring us to an island!" Ariki cried.

"Yes," Ipo replied, "and if we don't do something fast, we'll be wrecked!"

There, just to the south, was the unmistakable silhouette of an island; one surrounded by a coral reef. A line of white showed where storm swells broke on the coral. Without the whale to keep them moving, they were being washed onto its sharp, stony teeth.

"Paddle!" yelled Ariki.

"What with?" Ipo shouted.

"You use the old rudder, I'll use my hands." Ariki thrust her arms into the water and Ipo did what

he could with the remains of the rudder, flailing against the push of the swell.

They had just enough power over the boat to turn her, and point her to a narrow gap in the reef – visible as a dark break in the line of white foam.

"When the next swell rises, paddle hard," Ariki called. "We can make it if we don't get caught in the backwash."

They paddled until their muscles screamed. In the dark, it was hard to see what the water was doing, but they could feel it as it swirled and spun them around, then shot them forward. Ariki could just make out the calm, safe water of the lagoon in front of them, almost within reach. Then the swell was over and the water rushing back over the reef, taking them with it. The rear of the boat was wrenched sideways and the outrigger caught on a coral head. Once more, *Sea Beauty* flipped over, catapulting the three exhausted passengers out. Ariki landed beyond the reef in the lagoon, but when she got her head above the surface there was no sign of Ipo, Bad Boy or *Sea Beauty*.

She swam up and down, searching for her friends – but it was hopeless. Her strength gave out entirely, and it was all she could do to get to the shore. Shivering, utterly exhausted, she crawled up the beach to the dry sand, pulled some dry palm fronds over herself, and slept.

CHAPTER 5

The sun was already past its height when Ariki woke, almost delirious with thirst. The tinkling sound of running water nearby filled her mind. She scrabbled between trees and found a small stream tumbling over the rocks and collecting in pools of clear water. She fell to her knees and gulped straight from the stream. Nothing had ever tasted so good, but although her thirst was quenched her head still throbbed. She sat against a rock and closed her eyes.

"Mweep! Mmweeep!" said a voice.

Ariki looked around. Palms and ferns sprouted everywhere. The trunks of huge trees, of a kind she had never seen before, were dotted with oozing drops of golden resin that gleamed like jewels in the sunlight.

"Mweep! MWEEEEP!" said the voice again. She peered into the deep green shadows to see who or what was calling to her, and a head with a pair of luminous purple eyes poked out from behind a tree.

Ariki blinked to make sure she wasn't seeing things. It was a bird's head, she could tell that from the big yellow beak … but surely no bird could have a head bigger than a coconut?

"Mweep?" said the creature again. "Mweep?" And it stepped out from behind the tree. It was taller than she was, with the huge head balanced on a long, skinny neck and a big egg-shaped body, which was supported by a pair of sturdy yellow legs. It was covered in glossy blue feathers, with a tail fan of huge, stiff purple ones that matched its eyes. Frothy orange plumes sprouted from its head and the little stumps that were all it had for wings.

Fascinated, Ariki followed as the bird walked between the trees to where a space had been cleared and pressed flat, as if by the constant treading of many feet. In the middle was a strange construction made of sticks. Two rows of thin branches had been stuck into the ground so that their curved ends met and formed an arch, with a space between just big enough to walk through. Pebbles had been carefully arranged to mark the passage down the centre of the arch. It looked as if it had been prepared for some sort of ceremony.

The Mweep bird was now pushing sticks into the soft ground to add to the "arch" – so this was not human-made, but bird-made!

While Ariki was wondering if it was some kind of nest, the bird began to pull glossy blue feathers from its own body. One by one, it carried them to the nearest tree and dipped the shaft in the golden resin, then stuck the feather to the arch.

Satisfied at last with the decoration of its arch, the bird began to dance, dipping its head, waving its silly orange feathers and "mweep-mweeping" very loudly. Ariki realised that this was a male bird and the decorated arch was meant to impress females. She had seen male frigatebirds showing off their big red chests to do the same thing.

The bird danced through the arch and out again, shaking his orange plumes and pointing his beak towards her, screeching louder and louder, ending with a deafening shriek. Then, quite suddenly, he tucked his head under one fluffy wing stump and fell asleep. In seconds he was snoring.

The show was over – time for Ariki to begin her search. Her head was clear now, and she could remember the events of last night's wreck. As she made her way back through the trees and onto the beach, she willed her two friends to be waiting safely on the sand.

She shaded her eyes from the late afternoon sun and looked out over the bay. The lagoon lapped against a long, curved strand, made from sand as grey as ashes. Above it, the land climbed steeply and was covered in dense forest. It was a different sort of island altogether from the ones she was used to.

Halfway along the beach, she found a square of palm matting with two strings on either side – Ipo's improvised sunhat. Then, at the very end where it met an outcrop of boulders, she spotted *Sea Beauty*: still in one piece. The people who lived on the island must have dragged it up the beach and stowed it neatly in the shade of the leaning palm trees.

Ariki ran towards it, sure that she would find her friends resting in the shadows with their rescuers.

But the tracks around *Sea Beauty* told another story. There were deep imprints of large feet ... but feet without toes, quite unlike any Ariki had ever

seen. The only sign of Ipo was the faint imprint of
his feet, as if he had landed on the sand like a bird
and immediately taken off again. And the only sign
of Bad Boy was a long swirl of sand that showed
that something about the size of a small pig had
been dragged along beside the boat.

Ariki stared at the marks in the sand while fear
leaked into her heart. It looked as if some strange
creature, something big and very strong, had pulled
the boat from the water then carried her two friends
off. Whatever had happened, her only choice was to
follow where the trail led.

Soon she found herself on a well-worn path that ran through the forest along the edge of the island. The blue of the sea showed through the trees to her left, while to her right plants tangled over rocks and boulders. She stopped and listened; there were no voices calling, no sounds of singing or hammering as there would have been on Turtle or Big Toe. There were no human sounds at all, just little birds flitting in the treetops and the small, dry rustle of green lizards chasing over the rocks. Fairy terns flew past her, almost brushing her face with their wings; tropicbirds stared calmly from their nests at the base of trees and butterflies flashed their wings in patches of sunlight.

Cautiously, Ariki followed the path into a long tunnel of leaves and branches. Up ahead, it opened out into a clearing where sunlight splashed – and something was moving.

She crept along, careful to keep in the deepest

shadows, and peeped through the gaps between the leaves. The "something" was a person, but not like any kind of person Ariki had ever seen before. He was extremely tall and wide, and his body was almost entirely covered in very strange clothes. Where his hand peeped out, his skin was almost as pale as Ipo's; clearly without the clothes it would burn. His feet were covered in clothes too, bound up so that his toes were invisible. (How could you walk with your toes covered?)

But it was his face that was strangest of all: it was surrounded by bright orange hair and a beard, in the middle of which were two eyes the colour of the sea. The tangle of hair and the brightness of his eyes gave the man a fierce, wild look.

He was busy cooking something in a pot over the fire, and singing a song to himself in a very peculiar language, not one word of which Ariki understood.

"My yowie wi the crookit horn,
My yowie wi the crookit horn."

He was cutting up roots and dropping them into the pot, using a knife that looked as if it was made of moonlight – silver and shiny. Judging by the speed with which it chopped, it was impossibly sharp. Ariki was fascinated; she had never seen a knife such as that before.

Carefully, she moved a little closer – but a loud "mweep-mweep" sounded behind her, and a large feathery body ran into her, knocking her over. Ariki rolled like a coconut right to the feet of the strange, orange-bearded man.

She looked up into his face and decided that he was indeed very big, and very frightening. Did huge orange-bearded giants eat people? Was that the reason she had not heard another human voice on the island so far?

But the "mweep" bird wasn't afraid of him at all. In fact, he seemed very pleased indeed to see him and danced round, fluttering his silly stubby wings and trying to wind his long neck around the man's arm.

"Mweep, stop," the man told the bird – and, disentangling himself from Mweep, stepped towards Ariki. Ariki shut her eyes and expected to be sliced to bits with the shiny knife. But instead he leaned down and pulled her gently to her feet with one of his enormous hands.

"Greeting!" he said, giving a small bow. "Greeting very much. Happy-hearted me am to see more peoples."

He spoke in such a peculiar way, and with such a peculiar accent, that Ariki wasn't quite sure what he was saying. At least now that he was smiling, his face looked kind rather than terrifying.

"Bird hurt you?" the man asked, pointing to the

big bird. "Is Giant Bowerbird. Is called "Mweep" because he say own name all the time. Hatch from egg in my hands. He not mean hurt."

Ariki could only stare stupidly and smile.

"Ah," said the man. "Move after me, me have good thing for you eyes."

He led her across the clearing to a large but rather rickety hut, which stood with its back to the hillside.

The hut had a big, shaded veranda, and hanging from its roof were hundreds of little cages made of twigs and woven grass. Inside all of them, birds tweeted and lizards scuttled. Stacked against the wall of the veranda were yet more containers of a kind Ariki had never seen: small clear tubes, as if made of solid air, with beetles and spiders scrabbling inside.

"Prisoners," the man told her sadly, but he brightened immediately. "For small time only. Me picture them, then they are free!" And he opened his hands in the air like fluttering birds and laughed with such delight Ariki found herself smiling too.

She really had no idea what he was talking about, but suddenly that didn't matter. Nothing mattered, because there, inside the dark of the hut, fast asleep on a bed of mats and blankets, were Ipo and Bad Boy.

CHAPTER 6

Ariki was far too excited to let them sleep.

"Ah," said Ipo calmly, as he opened his eyes and saw her. "I thought it would take more than that to drown a Star Walker."

Bad Boy rubbed his nose against Ariki's legs. "Snnnnnnrrttt! Snnnnnnrrrrt!"

Ipo explained that the sea had flipped *Sea Beauty* back the right way up almost at once, and he had scrambled back on board and managed – just – to pull Bad Boy after him.

"I came straight up to the surface when we

capsized," Ariki told Ipo, "but I couldn't see you or the boat anywhere."

"There was no sign of you either," Ipo said, "and then we just drifted into the shore."

He and Bad Boy had collapsed exhausted on the boat, where the man had found them at first light.

"He's been very kind," said Ipo, "even though he looks so strange. I couldn't walk and he carried me and Bad Boy all the way here. He gave us food and water and made us comfortable."

The man seemed almost as pleased to see the friends reunited as they were themselves.

"Introducings now need," he announced. He pointed to himself. "Name me 'Crusoe McRobinson'. Me home Scotland, island big as the world. People ride there on giant pig. Travel much in this sea. Learn good your language." Here, he gave the very smallest swagger of pride. Then he pointed to the children. "You?"

Ariki was beginning to get used to Crusoe McRobinson's funny way of talking. In fact it was a bit catching, and she found herself saying, "Me name 'Ariki'. Me home Turtle Island. No giant pig there."

Ipo dug her in the ribs with his elbow and gave her a disapproving look. As Turtle Island's master outfitter and artist, he'd had a lot more experience of talking to people politely than Ariki had.

He stood up and returned Crusoe McRobinson's deep bow. "My name is Ipo. We are both from Turtle Island, far to the east. Our boat was caught in a storm and ..." Ipo paused. "Should I tell him about the whale?" he breathed.

Ariki shook her head. She wasn't sure bearded giants knew the stories about Paikea.

"... and we lost our sail and paddles," Ipo concluded.

"Also me," said Crusoe McRobinson. "Boat sink. I swim, others drown."

He sighed, then looked hopefully at Bad Boy.

"We will eat your pig?" he asked.

Horrified, Ariki and Ipo shook their heads.

"This is not an ordinary pig!" Ariki exclaimed. "He is..." She was struggling for a word to describe all the things that Bad Boy was.

Ipo stepped in. "He is special. He is *magic*!"

They all turned to Bad Boy, whose face was now covered in mud and who was chomping with an open mouth on a large, juicy worm. He looked very far from magic.

"Ah," said Crusoe, looking rather disappointed. "Then we will have other breakfast."

Although it was far too late in the day for breakfast, that seemed like a very good idea to everyone.

Crusoe McRobinson's camp was very well organized. A clear spring spurted out of the rocks to one side providing constant fresh water, and a second hut held supplies of food. Breakfast turned out to be something that he called "porridge". It didn't look very appealing – "rather like lumpy snot" was what Ipo said – but it tasted surprisingly good. Bad Boy wasn't interested in it; he was already finding his own food, pushing his snout happily between the roots and rocks and munching on all kinds of piggy delicacies, both plant and animal.

Mweep found the small pig fascinating. He approached Bad Boy, his head low, making soft cheeping sounds and fluttering his stumpy wings. The humans watched as pig and bird examined each other, beak to nose. Then, as if some agreement had passed between them, they began poking about in the dead leaves and soil together. Every time Bad Boy pulled something out of the earth – a root or a worm – Mweep pushed in a large nut.

"Why is he planting the nuts like that?" Ariki asked.

"To keep safe. Eat later," said Crusoe, adding, with a big smile, "but Bowerbird forget many seed. Seed grow to tree. Without Bowerbird plant and forget, tree will not grow. No tree from seed, no insect, no little bird. Giant Bowerbird magic, like your pig! Giant Bowerbird make all forest on island."

Suddenly Crusoe's expression changed, as fast as a breeze blowing over the sea. His smile was replaced with something that looked very much like fear.

What could such a big strong man be afraid of? Ariki wondered.

"Many Mweep dead," he whispered. "*Dog* kill."

Crusoe McRobinson said the word "dog" with a shudder in his voice.

"What is 'dog'?" Ariki breathed.

"I don't know," Ipo looked at the big man's frightened face, "but I don't think it can be anything very nice."

"When my boat sink," Crusoe explained, "all dead but me and *dog*. Dog bad, bad, bad. Come at night. Kill everything. Kill Bowerbird most of all."

The big man looked almost ready to cry, but just as quickly his expression changed again.

"This island full of creature. More creature than any land I see," he said, his eyes shining. "Creature *beautiful*! All live on big trees, and big trees grow because Bowerbird plant seed. Without Bowerbird, all life finish."

Just like an excited six-year-old, he jumped up and took the children by their hands.

"Come! Look!" he cried, pulling them to a table that stood on one end of the veranda. Crusoe opened a leather binder to reveal a stack of pale sheets – like the bark cloth on which Ipo painted his designs, but much stiffer and finer.

On every one was a picture, a perfect portrait of an animal. There were lots of Mweep's relatives – the males dancing round their bowers, the females drab and dull without the blue and orange feathers, and little fluffy long-legged chicks. But there were many, many other kinds of creatures, too. Birds of every colour with beaks in all kinds of shapes: curved up, curved down, pointed, round, long and short. Beetles with horns on their shells, with short legs and long legs, with long noses and eyes on stalks; lizards with stripes and spots, and some that looked exactly like leaves.

The children had never seen, never dreamed of, so many creatures on the land.

"So many kind of creature only live here, on this island. Nowhere else," Crusoe told them, beaming proudly – as if every animal was his own child. "Many creature need trees and trees need Mweep.

But dog kill many Mweep. Mweep almost gone." The big man's eyes filled with tears. He brushed them away with the back of his hand and showed the children more of his paintings.

In the golden light of late afternoon, the pictures glowed; each animal seemed so alive, as if at any minute they might get up and walk off the pages. The children stared at them in wonder.

Ipo was particularly impressed. "How did you do these?" he whispered. "It's as if the creatures are here, on these sheets!"

In answer, Crusoe opened a wooden box. Inside were brushes and pens, and little blocks of all kinds of colours. Ipo gasped.

"This my work. Work of my whole life," said Crusoe. "One day, all creatures on this island in pictures. This my dream."

Crusoe's extraordinary pictures told the children much more than

his odd words could. There were pictures of other men dressed like himself, of the "giant pig" on which his countrymen rode, whose real name was "horse". There were pictures of the enormous boat on which he had sailed the oceans. It was bigger than fifty of the

biggest boats that the children had ever seen, with great white sails like the wings of a huge seabird. Crusoe had made pictures of his

homeland, too; of hills and mountains, a land so large that no matter where you stood you could not see the ocean.

As he turned the pages, showing one image after another, Ariki was filled with astonishment and wonder. She had thought the world was made of ocean, but these pictures showed it was something else.

"Where is your land?" she asked, expecting Crusoe to point in a particular direction and tell her which stars he would follow to find his way home. Instead the man's eyes once more filled with tears.

"Me not know," he said. "Lost! Lost here on a lost island."

It was strange to hear a grown-up say that they were lost; for a Turtle Islander to be lost was shameful, something they would never admit to. Ariki felt sorry for Crusoe – although she had never been so far from Turtle Island before, she could point in the direction where it could be found: east towards the rising sun.

But she understood what it felt like not to know where your home was. Turtle Island was not where she had been born. That place was unknown to her, as lost to Ariki as Scotland and its "giant pigs" were to Crusoe McRobinson.

The sun had dropped into the sea and the shadows were growing, but Crusoe's camp was lit with a strange light. The rocks beside the spring were covered in tiny toadstools that began to glow a faint green as it grew dark. The children had seen sea creatures glowing with the same light, but never on the land. Crusoe collected one or two toadstools and placed them in one of his clear containers, which were called "glasses", to provide a lantern. Ariki and Ipo began to feel that they had been very lucky indeed to have found such an amazing island, with its glowing toadstools, Giant Bowerbirds and strange orange-bearded protector.

But, as the first stars came out, the peace of the camp was torn apart by a long, high howl that made their skin crawl. Mweep began to "mweep-mweep" in a small, anxious voice and drew very close to Crusoe, who turned even paler behind his red beard.

"Dog," he breathed. "And dog do this." Crusoe rolled up his sleeve and showed his white forearm. It was covered in horrible scars. It was clear that an animal big and brave enough to attack such a big strong man must be an absolutely terrifying creature. With a shaking hand, he reached among his store of pictures, drew one out and showed it to them in the toadstool-glow.

"Dog," he said, pointing to the creature in the picture.

Ipo had been right; "dog" certainly didn't look nice. It had four legs like a pig, but much longer and

more springy-looking. It had
a furry black coat and a huge
tail. But the scariest part was
its face – a long pointy nose,
fierce yellow eyes and the most
horrifying set of teeth, which
it was showing off in a very
unfriendly snarl.

"Oh," said Ipo. "How big is dog?"

"Big," Crusoe said. "Very." And he spread his arms
wide, indicating a beast four times the size of even
the biggest pig.

As if the creature knew it was being talked about,
it howled again. Crusoe McRobinson looked terrified.
"Help, please?" he asked. "We must build up fire. Dog
not like flames."

The children did as Crusoe asked while he blocked
off the pathways into the clearing with screens of
wood and palm leaves.

"We need to get off this island!" said Ipo, as they dragged a huge branch onto the fire.

"We must help him first," Ariki replied. "We can't just leave him with this dog thing. Anyway," she added, "if we help him get rid of the 'dog', he might help us repair *Sea Beauty* and get food and water for the voyage home."

The dog gave another bloodcurdling howl – thankfully from a bit further away.

"What can we do about a big fierce beast like that?" Ipo hissed.

"I don't know." Ariki grinned. "But you're forgetting that I can talk to giant sharks!"

CHAPTER 7

They slept inside the hut. Mweep slept standing on one leg with his head under his wing. Ariki, Ipo and Bad Boy huddled together in a corner. Ariki dreamed of pointy-nosed giants with huge teeth. But in the morning the terror of the dog seemed to have passed, and Crusoe sang his silly song as he made them more porridge.

"My yowie wi the crookit horn,
My yowie wi the crookit horn."

He had many barrels of the grey meal he used to make it, which he had saved from his ship when it went down, along with his paints and brushes and the white sheets he called "paper", which were stored inside big sheets of oiled cloth. Ariki felt sure that he must have some of the lovely white sails that they had seen in his pictures. Just a small section of one of those would replace the sail they had lost and get them home.

While the children ate, Crusoe McRobinson fed and watered all the creatures in the cages. Ariki noticed that he knew what every single one wanted and spent ages talking to and fussing over them. His big hands were so gentle, and he whispered to each creature as he tended to it. Then he took several of the cages to his desk and got out his brushes and pens.

"Now, me work," he called out to the children. "Later, talk."

He bent over his sheets in intense concentration. Ipo was fascinated and Crusoe didn't seem to mind being watched.

"I can mend my clothes at the same time," Ipo said. "Then I'll go and look for trees I can use for bark-cloth sail-making."

"And I'm going to look for dog," Ariki said. Ipo looked horrified. "Only joking! I'll go and check the damage on the boat and find something to make paddles out of. Maybe collect some coconuts. Perhaps we can ask Crusoe for some porridge?"

Ipo gave Ariki a stern look. They both knew that no one on Turtle Island would ever ask for something from a stranger without offering something bigger in return.

"No," he said. "We can get off this island without help and without battling monsters."

Ariki didn't reply. "C'mon," she said to Bad Boy. "Let's go."

She set off back down the path towards the beach, thoughts bouncing around her head like ripples from a hundred different islands. The "dog" creature sounded pretty fierce, but she wondered if it was really as bad as Crusoe said. Why would any ship, even a ship as big as the one in Crusoe's pictures, have such a dangerous animal on board? Perhaps "dog" was much bigger in Crusoe's head than it was in real life.

As she trotted down the path and looked around her, Ariki had to admit that what he said was true: the island was very, very full of life. She spotted six different kinds of butterfly – each one lovelier than the last – several kinds of lizards, and heard too many different bird-calls to count.

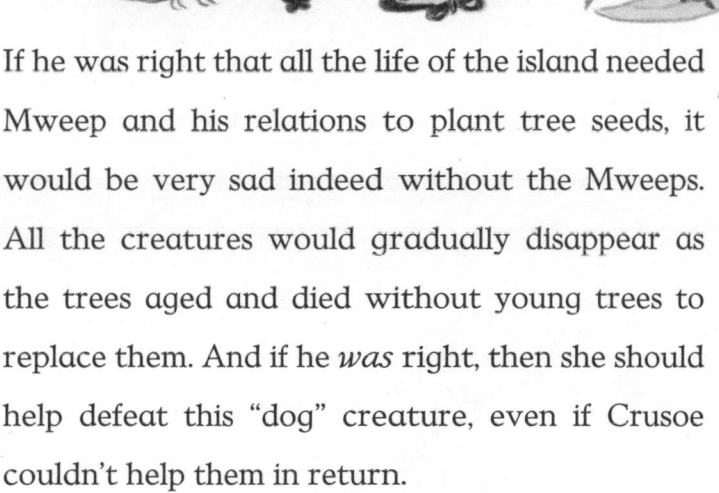

If he was right that all the life of the island needed Mweep and his relations to plant tree seeds, it would be very sad indeed without the Mweeps. All the creatures would gradually disappear as the trees aged and died without young trees to replace them. And if he *was* right, then she should help defeat this "dog" creature, even if Crusoe couldn't help them in return.

The night-time rain had left the plants sparkling with jewelled droplets; Ariki breathed deeply, and in among the sweet green smell of life was another less pleasant scent: blood.

Up ahead was a pile of bloody feathers. A dead Mweep lay on the path. Its long neck was broken, its lovely purple eyes misted over and its body

eaten away. It must have been killed by "dog" sometime in the night. Bad Boy squealed in alarm and stood back.

"It's all right, Bad Boy," Ariki reassured him. "I know it's horrible, but we need to take a closer look."

She checked the ground around for tracks; but the dead leaves showed no sign of huge paw-prints. And surely an animal such as the one Crusoe described would eat a dead Mweep in a few bites, not gnaw on it a bit. She was just concluding that maybe dog *wasn't* such a scary opponent when...

"Grrrrrrrrrrrrr!"

It wasn't a very loud noise, but it was full of threat – low and angry. Slowly, she turned round.

Standing on the path behind her was dog ... or rather, two "dogs".

They weren't anything like as big as Crusoe's stretched arms had suggested; not even as big as a full-grown pig. But they were four times as fierce as his picture had shown them to be. Their eyes gleamed with determination and their black fur stood on end. They bared their teeth and snarled.

"Snnrt!" said Bad Boy, his voice high with fear.

It was clear that the dogs were *very* interested in him. His stocky little body would make a much better meal than a whole flock of bony Mweeps. Ariki wished she had her spiked fishing spear; it would be perfect for keeping these creatures at bay. Step by step they came closer, waiting for their chance like hunting sharks.

Ariki knew they would wait for her attention to slip and then attack, but she risked a swift glance to her right. A long fallen branch lay beside the path, just within reach if she could move fast enough.

"Get ready, Bad Boy," she breathed. "Stay close."

He didn't need telling; he was already almost stuck to her ankles.

Very slowly, Ariki stepped sideways, edging towards the branch and beginning to bend her knees to drop her hand towards it. All the time she kept her feet ready for flight, balanced for the fastest sprint. She felt her toe hit the branch – then, in one, smooth movement, she snatched it up and swung it at the dogs. They weren't expecting a fight and they fell back just a little: enough to give Ariki and Bad Boy a head start.

Together they shot down the path, but the dogs were good runners; they caught up almost at once. At the top of the beach, Ariki was forced to turn and face them.

"Get behind me," she told Bad Boy. She held out the branch, lunging at the dogs to keep them back.

Little by little – with Bad Boy behind her – she backed down the beach. The dogs tried to split up and attack from opposite sides so one of them could run in and grab Bad Boy, but each time Ariki managed to stop them with a sharp stab of the branch. Dogs, it seemed, were not so tough after all.

But they snapped their teeth on the branch, and

she saw the strength of their jaws. If one of them got hold of her or the piglet, they'd have little chance of escape.

At last, Ariki felt her feet in the sea. As always, she felt instantly better. Water was her world. There was a stiff breeze blowing, whipping the lagoon into waves that smashed around her knees. She saw at once that the dogs didn't like it at all.

"Swim, Bad Boy, swim!"

Quite at home in the waves, the pig set off.
Ariki kept backing into the water and, as soon as
she was deep enough, she swam, too. The dogs
began to follow, but they were not confident
swimmers. They strained to keep their noses out
of the waves and their eyes turned white with fear
when water washed over them.

Ariki and Bad Boy swam out, bobbing in the lagoon beyond the zone where the waves broke. Soon the dogs turned back. For a while they stood on the shore, snarling and trying to bite the waves. At last they ran off and disappeared into the forest.

Ariki watched from the water for a while. At the highest point of the island, the trees grew more thinly and, after a few minutes, she spotted the two creatures running along a rocky ridge, heading away.

You aren't going to kill any more Mweeps, she told them in her head. *I know* two *things you're afraid of now – fire and water!*

CHAPTER 8

Back on land, Ariki found she was a little nervous and kept looking over her shoulder and listening for growling. So it took her longer than she had expected to check the boat over, do what she could to repair any damage, and make a list in her head of all they needed to get home: a new rudder and two paddles; rope and a new sail.

It was a short list, but it would take a long time to replace these items – especially here, on an island where none of the trees or plants were familiar. On Turtle Island she would have known the right trees or fallen branches to make a paddle, the right palm leaves to shred and bind to make rope ... but here, everything was unfamiliar. She wondered if Ipo had found a tree with the right bark for sail-making.

Before leaving the beach, she swam out over the lagoon with a stick she had rubbed to a point using a rock: a makeshift fishing spear. Porridge was all right, but she wanted to catch some fish for their next meal. But she found that even the ocean here was different. None of the many fish that swam in the lagoon were familiar, and she had no idea how to tell which were good to eat. Some fish on the reefs around Turtle Island were poisonous and everyone learned, very young, to keep away from them.

In the end she settled for some that looked a bit like Blush Fish. They had the same rounded bodies and the same pink skin – the only difference Ariki noticed was a line of little blue spines along their backs. When she brought the three she had speared back to shore, she wrapped them carefully in layers of leaves to keep the spines from scratching her. Then she set off up the long path, listening out for any following footsteps that were not Bad Boy's.

When she got back to the camp, there was no one there. The fire had burned down to a faint glow, the paints, pictures and brushes were all packed away, and the hut was closed. There was no sign of Crusoe, Mweep or Ipo.

She decided to wait until they returned to cook their meal, so she put the parcel of fish in the shade, collected some more firewood, and sat down to wait, while Bad Boy stretched out in a little patch of sunshine and began snoring.

"Wake up, Ariki." Ipo was shaking her hard. The look on her friend's face told her something was very wrong.

"What's happened?"

Ipo was very out of breath and struggled to speak. "Crusoe took me to see the last Mweep birds," he explained. "I think he planned to round them up somehow, and bring them here to keep safe. But the dogs chased them all across the island. Not just one dog, but lots. They aren't big but..."

"I know. I've seen two of them," Ariki interrupted.

"They've got the Mweeps trapped, and Crusoe is trying to protect them – but he's almost frozen with fear. He needs help."

Ariki leaped up. "I thought you didn't want to help him," she said.

"I changed my mind," said Ipo. "He's so kind. He asked about my skin and he gave me this. It's called a 'shirt'." He pointed to the big white garment he was wearing. "But we have to hurry, Ariki, this is an emergency!"

Ariki nodded. "Okay, then put some of the embers in that cooking pot. We'll need to make a fire, fast." She grabbed her sharpened stick and the parcel of fish.

"What's that?" Ipo asked.

"Bait," she replied – then she gave the still-sleeping pig a shove with her foot. "Come on, Bad Boy, time to run."

Shaking the dreams from his ears, the pig trotted after them, up the path that led through the forest to the rocky ridge at the top of the island.

They ran hard, too hard to talk, with Ipo leading the way. Ariki noticed that his "shirt" worked very well – it was so large it covered him from neck to knees, and cast enough billowing shade to keep most of the sun off his shins and feet too. He still wore the same "hat", the scrap of matting from *Sea Beauty*, although it had a neat new piece of rope tying it to his head.

The path snaked steeply up the hillside, through great groves of trees and out onto a rocky ridge where patches of flowers coloured the hillside blue and purple, pink and yellow.

At last, Ipo stopped and pointed. They were looking down, over the far side of the island, which was steeper and rockier than the side where Crusoe had his camp. Cliffs and crevices fell straight into wild, open ocean and deep ravines sliced down into the waves.

Just below where they stood, on the end of a

narrow finger of rock, a little group of giant birds was standing very close together; there were two males and three smaller females. Together, the last of their kind. All of them were crying out in anguish, a chorus of "mweep-mweeping". The rock was surrounded by a steep drop on three sides so the flightless birds would stand no chance if they were to jump. Cutting off their escape was a group of dogs, led by a big grizzled female with four younger dogs behind her. The only thing between the Mweeps and the dogs was Crusoe McRobinson, with his pet Mweep right behind him, calling plaintively.

Crusoe was holding his long knife out in front of him, and waving it at the dogs. But he was no fighter, and even from this distance the children could see that he was very afraid. He looked as if he might drop the knife at any moment – and then the dogs would attack. There was no time to lose.

"We can't take on that lot with one sharpened stick," Ipo said.

"No ... but I can get them to come after me, instead of the birds and Crusoe." Ariki had noticed that just before they reached the narrow strip where the Mweeps and Crusoe were trapped was the entrance to a deep gully, and a clump of dead trees – dry and ready to burn.

"Quick!" she said. "We need to get to those trees and light a fire."

"Hold on, Crusoe!" Ipo yelled, but the breeze carried his voice away, back down the path they had already taken.

It took seconds to get to the trees, but it seemed like hours. Down there, they could no longer see the dogs or the birds; but they could hear the terrified "mweep-mweep" calls.

"As long as we can still hear them," Ariki said, "we've got time."

Ipo was hastily gathering strands of dry grass and adding them to the embers. Flames leaped up in moments. He added twigs and bits of dry branch that lay around under the trees.

Ariki handed over the fish. "We need to cook these."

"Why?" Ipo asked.

"We're downwind of the dogs, so as soon as they smell the fish they'll come this way; then Bad Boy and I will lead them down there." She pointed into the shadow of the gully.

"And then what?" said Ipo.

"You set light to these trees. The dogs will be trapped between the sea and the fire."

The fish began to sizzle and the strong, delicious scent was snatched up by the wind. Ariki was betting that the dogs had not smelled anything so good for a long time. (She rather thought the same herself.)

"What happens then?"

"I'm not sure, but it will get the dogs away from Crusoe and the Mweeps."

"What about you?"

Ariki grinned. "Oh, that's easy. They don't like swimming!"

The dogs began to howl as they smelled the fish. Ariki speared the leafy packet with her sharp stick and ran towards the mouth of the gully.

"Be ready to light the trees," she called over her shoulder as she dropped over the edge, with Bad Boy following fearlessly behind her.

The gully was steep and full of fallen rocks that slid and shifted under Ariki's feet. But if it was hard for her, it would be hard for the dogs, too. Bad Boy's little trotters were surprisingly good at getting him from one rock to the next, and he was soon ahead of her. Ariki was careful to drop juice from the part-cooked fish to give the dogs a clear trail. They'd follow the scent, then, at the end of the gully, there would be the sea. She and Bad Boy would swim away, but the dogs would be trapped between water and fire. It wasn't a permanent solution to Crusoe's problem, but at least it would give him the chance to get the Mweeps to safety.

The howling had stopped and she could hear the dogs' panting and the clack of their claws on the rocks above her. Pebbles bounced and slid as they hurried towards the delicious smell. The deeper she went, the narrower the gully grew.

Ariki glanced back. The first dog was perhaps

five canoe-lengths behind her. That was too close, but the ravine was so narrow that they would have to come down one by one, and if they attacked they couldn't do it all together. That was good, but she didn't want to find out how long her rough stick-spear would hold them off. She just wanted to get to the sea so she and Bad Boy could swim out of trouble.

Quite suddenly, and unexpectedly, the gully flattened out.

Ariki felt her stomach clench. The ravine didn't go down to the sea. It didn't go anywhere.

She had run into a dead end, and there was no escape.

CHAPTER 9

Frantically Ariki looked up at the steep walls of smooth rock, which rose all around. They leaned in a little, so that the very end of the gully ran under an overhang of rock. There was no way she could climb out, even without Bad Boy. And there wasn't going to be any rescue; the smell of burning wood filled the air and smoke cloaked the narrow band of sky she could see as she peered upwards. Ipo had done exactly what she asked. Now no one could get in or out of this trap without walking through fire.

Ariki set her back against the rock and pushed

Bad Boy in behind her legs. She held out the packet of fish on the stick. It might buy them just a little more time.

The first of the dogs stepped from between the boulders into the small sandy space where Ariki stood. It was the big female. Close up, Ariki could see that she was old and thin, and that some of her teeth were broken. Her eyes flashed when she saw the dripping packet of fish *and* the pig.

The next dog – a male, younger but smaller – squeezed in beside her. Their tongues lolled and their noses sniffed the air. Soon the others were jostling for position behind them, so close they were like one creature, hairy and panting and hungry.

They moved closer and closer. Bad Boy began to squeal. Ariki let them get almost within reach of her stick-spear, then she threw the fish over their heads, aiming it low so they would see and smell it before it landed in among the last of the dogs.

It worked! The front dogs were wedged in so tightly between the walls of the gully that they bit and snarled at each other in their effort to turn round and get to the food. There was a horrible fight, but still every dog seemed to manage to gulp down a share of the fish, spines and all.

Ariki darted forwards and jabbed at the one nearest her. There was a panicked tangle of teeth and fur as the creature yelped in pain.

She jabbed hard at another dog then stepped back – but when she tried a third jab, one of the younger dogs grabbed her spear and snapped it.

Smoke was blowing down the gully from the burning trees. Ariki coughed and spluttered, and her eyes hurt. The dogs were frightened by the smell of fire, but their fear made them more aggressive and, with the fish gone, they wanted more to eat. Ariki looked down, searching for something – a rock or a pebble – to throw, but her fingers found only sand and dust.

The dogs stared past her legs to the cowering Bad Boy ... and drooled.

Then the first dog rushed in and closed its jaws round Ariki's arm. She hit it with her other fist and it let go, but the second dog had got a hold of Bad Boy. It was pulling him backwards while the other dogs were rearing up and snarling with frustration behind. Ariki grabbed the pig's back leg and pulled, while trying to jab at the dog with her foot. It let go and she shot back with the piglet on top of her.

There was nothing she could do now to defend herself.

"Yoooooowww!"

It wasn't a howl; it was more of a scream. For a moment, Ariki couldn't tell where it came from – and then she saw the dog at the back had green froth coming from its mouth. It yowled again and began to wobble on its legs, as if a giant invisible hand had got hold of it and was shaking it to pieces.

Then it dropped to the ground, its tongue lolling: quite dead.

The other dogs backed off, their eyes showing sudden fear. Another began to yowl, that same horrible sound, then another and another.

In seconds, every single one had dropped dead before her eyes.

Ariki stood and looked down at them. Bad Boy sniffed the remains of the leaves that had wrapped the fish, but she pulled him back. "That's what killed them – those fish must have been poisonous!"

Lying dead, the dogs didn't look at all frightening. Just skinny and sad. Ariki felt almost grateful to them: by eating the fish they had saved her life and Ipo's too.

"Without the dogs," Ariki told Bad Boy, "*we* would have eaten the fish – and died."

Above the gully, the smoke was thinning. The trees had burned more quickly than Ariki expected, and now the flames were dying down. As she walked up the ravine, rocks crackled and pebbles tumbled down, loosened by the heat of the fire; the trees were just blackened stumps against the blue sky. As she scrambled upwards she heard Crusoe McRobinson calling her name.

"Here! Here," she replied, and he gave a joyful shout – and then she heard Ipo call her name, too.

Three faces peered over the jagged lip of the gully: Ipo, Mweep and Crusoe.

"We feared!" said Crusoe. "We feared much." The big man leaned over the edge, and his long sinewy arms reached down and lifted Ariki out. She found her legs were a bit wobbly so Ipo held her steady for a moment.

Crusoe pulled Bad Boy out too and held him high. "Snnnrt," said the pig, and wiggled his ears.

Crusoe laughed, a great booming peal of mirth.

"Magic Pig. Yes, magic indeed!" he exclaimed, and put Bad Boy down next to Mweep's big yellow feet so the bird could inspect his friend.

The little group of surviving Mweeps was picking its way over the rocky ridge and back into the forest.

Crusoe watched them sadly. "Safe now," he said, "but how will I *keep* them safe? Where dog now?"

"Crusoe, the dogs are dead," Ariki told him. "The fish I gave them were poisonous."

Ipo gasped. "You didn't tell me that part of the plan!"

"It wasn't part of the plan – the plan was that those fish would be our dinner."

Crusoe stared at her, amazed. "Dog dead? All dog? All *five*?" he said.

Ariki nodded.

"Then Bowerbirds safe forever!" he spread his arms and beamed. "All island safe forever!"

"Unless there are more dogs..." said Ipo. "Look."

There was a movement under a bush, close to where the birds had wandered off between the trees. A tiny face looked out at them, then darted into the shadows when it realised it had been spotted.

They went over to investigate. Under the bush was a hole: a den. Inside was one baby dog – "pup", Crusoe called it. It was very small, very skinny and very afraid.

Ariki reached in and pulled it out. The pup whined miserably.

"I don't think it's had time to learn how to be fierce," said Ipo.

Ariki held it up and looked at its face. It wagged its tail and then licked her nose. She laughed and Crusoe shook his head and gently took the pup from her.

"I was small, like this pup," he explained, pointing to the old scars on his arms. "Big dog bite me, very bad. So all my life me fear dog … until now!"

And he laughed so much he had to sit down.

CHAPTER 10

After that, the young Turtle Islanders felt that it was all right to accept Crusoe's help and Crusoe was more than happy to do all he could to get them ready for their journey home. He had two good oars saved from his wrecked ship and he insisted that they take them. He had escaped in a rowing boat and when it broke up on the reef he and the oars had floated to shore.

The captain's pregnant dog had been the only other survivor. The tough old girl had swum ashore and given birth to her puppies, who had survived the only way they knew how. Fortunately, the last descendant of the captain's dog hadn't learned her family's fierce ways. She was a sweet-natured little thing who was completely terrified of the giant birds, and ran between Ariki's legs every time Mweep came near.

Crusoe gave Ariki and Ipo a barrel of porridge and, in return, Ariki showed him how to dive to find conch shells and other smaller shellfish. They were the same as the ones on Turtle Island, so she was sure they were safe to eat. Crusoe didn't want to kill anything in order to survive, but Ariki explained that there really were a lot of shellfish and one gingery man, no matter how large, would not be able to eat them all.

But Crusoe McRobinson could not help with the sail. All the sails on his ship had gone down with her, and a search of the island from end to end and side to side showed that there were no trees suitable for making bark-cloth. During their search, they came across Mweep's bower. Ipo looked at it very closely; he had the same expression on his face that he got when he was coming up with a new design.

"I've had a *really* good idea," he announced. "I can make a frame of twigs and stick feathers to it using the tree resin, just like Mweep did. Then a bit of stitching to make them firmer, then coat them in resin. It'll make a waterproof sail, even better than a bark-cloth one."

"I'd never have thought of that," said Ariki. "Master Tailor and Master Sail-Featherer!" She gave Ipo a deep, Crusoe-style bow.

They set to work at once, bending long, springy twigs and tying them with twisted grass to make a frame. Then came the feather-sticking. Mweep's arch was now almost covered in feathers, so Ariki and Ipo began to steal some to use for their sail. They had thought Mweep wouldn't mind or notice, but they were wrong. Almost as if he *felt* the children pulling them from his bower, he appeared out of the trees, "mweeping" furiously, and snatched a stolen feather from Ipo's hand.

Then the big bird turned his head upside down to inspect the feathers stuck to the sail frame. With a thoughtful "mweep", he disappeared into the trees. They could hear him calling somewhere off in the shadows, and in a few minutes he was back, his beak stretched wide around a huge bunch of feathers. They weren't the small blue ones he had used on his arch, but big purple ones, like the ones in his tail.

He dropped them at Ipo's feet and stood staring at them in silence, his head hanging, his bright orange plumes drooping. There were no feathers missing from his tail and in any case there were far, far too many to have come from his own body. Ariki guessed they must have belonged to his dead companions, killed by the dogs over the last year.

The bird raised his head. His huge purple eyes looked down the length of his beak.

"Mweep," said Mweep. Then he picked up one of the feathers and put it in Ipo's hand.

"Thank you, Mweep," said Ipo. "Are these the feathers of your family?"

"Mweep," the big bird said softly.

Ipo reached out and stroked the bird's soft, feathery cheek. "Well, no more birds are going to be killed. You're safe now, Mweep."

"And we'll take the little pup with us when we go," said Ariki, "just in case!"

Ipo sewed the big purple feathers in place, overlapping them like fish-scales, and then coated them with golden resin from the trees to make them stronger and more sea-proof.

As soon as the feather sail was ready they carried it to the boat and fixed it in place using the ropes that Crusoe had given them. A little trial journey over the lagoon showed that it would work well.

Crusoe helped them carry the barrel of porridge to the boat and gave them another barrel full of water, to add to their stores in the water gourds. He gave them a knife made of the same shiny stuff as his own.

"Iron," he told them. "Made from iron. Very sharp."

All that was left to do was to say goodbye.

They planned to start their journey at dusk, to set their course by the Sea Urchin and then the path of stars that pointed back to Turtle Island. Crusoe McRobinson and Mweep came down to the beach and helped them get *Sea Beauty* into the water. Bad Boy rubbed his nose against the big bird's beak and climbed aboard with Pup, who curled up in the cabin as if she'd been born on the sea.

"You could come with us," Ipo told Crusoe. "You could teach me how to make pictures like you do."

"Maybe you'd find your star path to Scot-lind," Ariki suggested.

The big man grinned. "My work *here*. Pictures make of all life." He spread his arms wide and laughed. "One year, two year, ten year, boat come. I see my land again then. Now, me happy! You be happy also."

The yellow gleam of the Sea Urchin was just peeping above the horizon. It was time to leave, but as they pushed the boat into the water Crusoe suddenly stopped.

"Wait! Wait!" he cried. "Me forget."

He took off up the beach back to his camp, and returned panting. He gave Ipo a small pot of blue pigment and a brush.

"I'll be famous for my blue designs," Ipo exclaimed, delighted. "Thank you, Crusoe."

Crusoe handed Ariki a flat leather folder. "Inside picture for you. A boy, from island of fire, far to west."

It was too dark now to look at this odd gift, and they were anxious to begin their journey. Ariki thanked Crusoe, and the man nodded solemnly before pushing them out into the lagoon. He stood watching them in the moonlight as Ipo took the rudder and Ariki turned the sail to catch the breeze and carry them from shore – through the channel in the reef, and out into the open ocean.

Soon all that was left of Crusoe McRobinson and his island of wonders was his voice, singing out over the water:

"My yowie wi the crookit horn,
My yowie wi the crookit horn."

CHAPTER 11

Every day the Star Walker, old Arohaka, had looked out to sea for his apprentice.

He would not believe the girl had been lost in the storm with her companion. Every day, he told Ipo's granny, "She will bring him back. She is a very important part of the ocean. Her soul knows more than I can teach her. She will find a way."

The old woman patted his hand and cried, and didn't believe him for a moment.

The Queen of Big Toe did not believe him either. Arohaka had had to give her his finest sow, the famous Pupuli, and all her latest litter of piglets, as compensation for the new sailing boat that his apprentice had stolen. The Queen's daughters, who had once said that they adored Ariki the Shark-Charmer, now said all sorts of very rude things about her. They even claimed that the Giant Shark story was just something the Turtle Islanders had made up.

Relations between Turtle Island and Big Toe had grown rather chilly. Queen Manatui, who had not always been Arohaka's friend or Ariki's supporter, broke off her engagement and cancelled the wedding feast!

Everyone missed Ariki and Ipo – not just Arohaka and Granny. They were sorry that these two rather unusual young people had been badly thought of in the past, and felt they had never really given them enough credit for their talents and exploits.

"And as for those girls of the Queen's…" they said. "Well, what do *they* know about anything?"

Without Ariki and Ipo, the island seemed a sadder place. People felt that perhaps nothing really interesting was ever going to happen to them again.

But then one morning, a toddler, up early and on the lookout for robber crabs to trap, told his ma he'd just heard some strange singing from a boat with a purple sail, coming up the Nose.

"My yowie wi the crookit horn,
My yowie wi the crookit horn."

Within half an hour, the whole island was celebrating the return of their heroes.

Ariki and Ipo were skinny, but otherwise in good health, and the stories they had to tell were amazing. The children were carried to the Gathering Hut, where the knife (made of "i-ron") was passed from hand to hand, and the "shirt" worn by Ipo much commented on.

It was Ipo who did most of the talking, giving an account of all that had befallen them. He seemed to have got taller during his absence, and had become a great storyteller: no one whispered round the back when he spoke (although the strange little creature who wagged its tail at everyone and tried to nibble people's toes was a bit distracting).

The whale rescuer, the giant birds, the marauding "dogs", Crusoe McRobinson, Scot-lind and the giant pigs, and all the other new stories, made the Turtle Islanders feel special again. Everyone agreed that visitors would be coming to hear all about Ariki and Ipo's new adventures.

"And that's before I've started making blue pictures," Ipo whispered to Ariki.

Ipo was so full of stories, and the Turtle Islanders were so busy listening to them, that it was only Arohaka who noticed the change in his apprentice.

"The ripples proved very useful, Star Walker," she told him respectfully, "and I'm very sorry about taking the boat and about Pupuli."

Arohaka smiled to himself. "Sorry" had not been a word in Ariki's vocabulary before.

"Well, those girls will tell that story for the rest of their lives," he said. "And no one else is sad to see the back of Pupuli. Big Toe doesn't know what it's in for! I always knew you would come back. I never doubted you: not for one second, Ariki."

"Thank you, Arohaka," said Ariki. (There was another new phrase, thought the Star Walker.) "But I won't be here for long."

"I think I knew that too." The old man sighed. "Where will you go?"

"I will search for the place I'm from," she answered. "And now I have another clue. Crusoe McRobinson gave me this."

Out of a leather pouch she drew a pale sheet, like bark cloth. On it was a picture that took Arohaka's breath away; it was so exact, so lifelike.

A boy stood there looking out at him from the white page.

"He has your tattoo!" Arohaka exclaimed.

"Crusoe made this picture," Ariki told him. "He said this boy lived on an island of fire far to the west. So that's where I will sail – to find him, and to find my true home."

Arohaka nodded. "You must follow your own path now, Ariki," he said. "You aren't an apprentice any more: you are a real Star Walker."